★ AN ★ AMERICAN CAROL

CHADWICK BICKNELL

DEFIANCE PRESS
& PUBLISHING

An American Carol

ISBN: 978-1-955937-56-6 (Paperback)
ISBN: 978-1-955937-55-9 (eBook)

Published by Defiance Press and Publishing, LLC

Bulk orders of this book may be obtained by contacting Defiance Press and Publishing, LLC. www.defiancepress.com.

Public Relations Dept. – Defiance Press & Publishing, LLC
281-581-9300
pr@defiancepress.com

Defiance Press & Publishing, LLC
281-581-9300
info@defiancepress.com

ACKNOWLEDGMENTS

I want to thank my family and friends who supported me in writing this novel. Politics is always divisive, and it makes me happy to realize everyone I know of different opinions was able to enjoy the story. This story isn't about politics but rather how we as people should be and I'm glad those I let preview could see that. A final thank you to everyone who is reading this book now. I hope you enjoy it!

The summer heat is always a scorcher in July. I wish I could say I was surprised, but all of the fossil fuel loving Ultra Conservatives are the reason it's so hot. They pollute our planet and make it uninhabitable. It won't be long before this beautiful earth is gone. That's why I am spending this 4th of July protesting the evil Conservative Party. They love the 4th of July like it is the second coming of Jesus. I hate it. I don't care about this country; I don't care about the "freedom" they claim we have. Tell that to all of the minorities who aren't enjoying the freedoms I get. I'm gay and I probably have it better than most minorities, but even I am still limited in what I can and can't do because of the Acers.

I used to love this holiday. I even used to follow

my parents beliefs politically, but as I grew to understand my own sexuality, I came to realize I wouldn't be accepted by my family. Yes they say they support me, but they vote for the party that opposes everything about me! It makes no sense. So I guess you can say I hardened my heart to everything the Conservative Party represents. I do everything I can to oppose them and it has gotten me allies and enemies. I haven't celebrated it in years and my parents have been trying to get me back to celebrating.

Instead I've spent the last several years ramping up my political involvement. It started in college when I met my then boyfriend Jack. I thought we were going to be together forever, but then things changed in our senior year in college. It was the year Ace won the Presidency. I remember that night so well. It's a nightmare I can never wake up from. Jack and I were living together. All of our friends came over to celebrate what we believed would be Hellen's well-deserved victory. She had a 100 percent chance of winning according to CNN. Yet Ace won.

I broke down. I knew it was the end of everything

my community had fought for. Jack tried to keep me strong but I couldn't help it. I couldn't accept Daniel Ace victory. I ramped up my protests everywhere. I joined local groups and let myself be heard. I joined protests in St. Louis, Missouri and burned entire buildings down. I didn't get caught. You might think that is violent and what if someone died? I say who cares. Anyone who is against what I believe is the enemy and deserves whatever comes their way.

Jack changed though. At first—before Ace—he was with me on everything, but then he began to question if our ways were wrong. I told him he was insane if he thought those disgusting Conservative Party people were any better. He finally broke up with me and moved out. I remember coming home and seeing his jeep and a trailer filled with stuff. I said *screw it* and let him leave. If he didn't want to defend our rights, then he was not the one for me.

In 2019 I opened my charity Rainbow Lance and began serious efforts across my home state of Missouri but also the nation to ensure the rights of my community. I have been very aggressive and it has made me disliked, even by people in my own line of thinking. Every year around this time, I see the weakness of my fellow progressives when they ask to be off for July 4th so they can be with their disgusting Conservative families or Democrat families who choose to ignore the disgusting nature of the holiday. I usually fire a few dozen people every year at this time. If you aren't committed to the cause, then I don't need you.

This year has been no different. I'm with my assistant Claire. She is asking about having the 4th off to celebrate at her boyfriend's family home. Obviously that can't happen because I have huge protests planned with some of the nation's top progressives. I try to let her down gently. I need her here to help organize everything. I just fired a dozen people over wanting the 4th fourth off, so now we are shorthanded. It's July 2nd and time is short for me.

"Sir, please. I haven't seen his family for months and they are already nervous given I work for you. I don't want them thinking I don't like or even want to see them because they voted for the Conservative Party. I have never asked for a day off. Please!" she pleads with me. I shake my head.

"Claire, if I work late, you work late. This is an important time in our mission to blue wave the country and you're a vital part of this!"

"I understand, but sir this is important."

I am very quick and to the point with my frustration. "Then you're fired," I say. Claire seems shocked. She asks if I'm serious. I reply she has five minutes to get her stuff and leave. With that, I point to the door and she leaves my office. Now I am sitting in my office finishing work that needs to be done. Since I am now out an assistant, I might as well go home and work there. I see Claire walk by later with a box of her things.

As I finish up and walk out of my office, I am stopped by a voice I really don't want to hear. "Alex! I've missed you little brother," Michael, my older brother, calls. He comes by and asks me to come to some family gathering every few months and I always say *no*. I want nothing to do with my family. They voted for Ace twice despite knowing I am gay. They claim to support me, but no one who votes for Ace can support me too.

"Not now Michael. I was just leaving and I am tired. If this is about the 4th, save it. The answer is *no*. I hate this holiday and I will be spending it doing what is right and that is protesting! The climate, gay rights, abortion, the fight never ends," I say.

My brother sighs at me. "I know. All you do is fight these days. You fight with me, Mom, Dad. We all love you and just want you to be with us. I know you don't like who we voted for but is that really a good reason to cut us out of your life? One day we'll be gone and you'll have no one but those who fear to displease you. Is that a life?" my brother rebuts. I clench my teeth.

"What do you know about it? Just leave me alone!" I shout and storm past him.

I don't bother to see my brother's expression because I want and need to get away so I can go home and finally relax. There are still a lot of things I need to plan for but I have time. Michael follows after me. I have to wait so I can lock up. He tries once more but I shoot him down again. He tells me what time everything will be starting if I change my mind. Same old brother. He thinks I will just change my mind. I'm not Jack. I don't forsake my kind.

You're probably wondering how you can be this hard headed over everything. Why so aggressive? My best friend Megan. She killed herself because she couldn't take what was happening to this planet and to everyone who wasn't white and a male or Conservative Party woman. She shot herself in front of me and it was with my gun. Well my brother's. He gave it to me when I opened the office in St Louis. He wanted me to be protected because the crime rate is high due to the Conservative Party making it hard on minorities. Not that only minorities do the crimes in St Louis. After that the gun was taken into evidence while her suicide was investigated. Once it was determined that I and no one else was at fault, I got the gun back. I buried it at my grandfather's the last time I was there. I couldn't stand to look at it.

Megan helped me get Rainbow Lance off the ground. Together we worked hard and we became so successful. I had a plaque installed above my office with her name and her favorite quote inscribed. "Well behaved women seldom make history." I missed her a lot. Her death was the straw that broke the camel's back in my life. I became a cold person after that, but I'm okay with it. Aggression gets things done. I don't care what evils I have to do to get what I want accomplished. It's for the betterment of the world, so that is all the justification I need.

I left my brother and got in my Tesla. I drove back to my apartment. It was on the top floor of one of the buildings in the city. The Arch was visible from it and I could spot parts of the river. I enjoyed the view a lot. I had hoped me and Jack would be enjoying the view at this point in our lives. Maybe even be married and have kids. That dream died six years ago though. I doubt I will ever get it back. Not that I wanted him back. Even if I did miss a lot of things about Jack. I could never take him back. He became the unthinkable. He became a gay Conservative, and I can't even begin to understand why.

The last time we spoke was when I saw that he had been working for an up-and-coming young congressman. I remember screaming at him so hard. He just listened to me and let me. I wouldn't even listen to him when he wanted to explain himself. Not that there is anything that can justify such a betrayal. I can't ever forgive him.

I pour myself a glass of wine and cook myself some dinner. I turn on my TV and put on the news so I can see what is being ruined now. In truth I should take a break because I get angry from the news, but given my job I have to be up to date on everything. I wish I could say my drinking habits were okay, but in truth I downed the bottle. I've been in a spiral for a while and have yet to climb out of it.

I pop a couple of muscle relaxers and another glass of wine and lie down on my couch and switch to a movie on Amazon. *After We Fell*. I love Hardin, so sexy. I fell asleep to the romance movie with an empty wine glass in my hand. I wish I could say I didn't do that often. Life happens and we drink wine. It worked out for the ancients. I didn't used to drink a lot, but between being eternally single, my friend's suicide a couple of years ago and the stress of my work, I need a drink or two or the bottle to relax for the night. I'm usually fine, but stress has been getting me lately.

I pull out my phone and see notifications on *Snapchat*. Looks like Jack updated his story. I blocked him from my life in every sense of the word. Except *Snapchat*. I hate to admit it, but I still think about him all the time and where we could be now. He dated someone for a little bit, but they broke up a year ago. Yes, I have been stalking the *Snapchat* and articles on him; sue me. He looks so good and happy. Why am I miserable and he is happy? I toss my phone down and reach for the bottle.

As I touch the bottle, the apartment begins to shake. The front door to my apartment begins to rattle hard. I can hear a loud humming. I back away further and yell for whoever it was to go away. "I'll call the cops! Leave now!" I yell once more. The door breaks open and a cloud of wooden shrapnel and dust envelopes my apartment.

As it clears I hear a raspy yet feminine voice. "Sorry about that." The thing walks toward my kitchen I think; the dust is super thick. "Do you mind? I'm going to have a drink," the female voice says. The dust settles and I can see a grayish woman going to my wine fridge. Several chains are wrapped around her and dragging behind as she walks. She opens the door and grabs a bottle. I am rightfully freaking out and start throwing toward her random things I can get my hands on. She grabs a glass and begins to pour herself wine. One of the objects I throw hits the glass and knocks it from her hand and onto the floor. It shatters.

"Dude! I don't mind you throwing shit at me but take it easy on the Merlot," she says. She then holds the bottle up. "I don't need a glass. You don't mind, do you?" I say nothing as the woman turns and drinks straight from the bottle. That's when it dawns on me. This thing. It looks like. "It can't be ... yo-you're dead!" I scream.

The woman drinks the whole bottle and tosses it to the floor. That's when I notice her face. Half of it is missing; it's a skeleton. The other half is of my friend. "I know. Right. You look good Alex." She walks toward me. I back away a little further which puts me against my large window.

"What are you doing here ... and as a zombie?" I ask. Megan walks closer. She spots a pack of cigarettes on the end table by my couch.

She picks them up. "You mind? Two years dead; you really miss the simple things. Booze, smokes, mashed potatoes."

God I think I am dying. Is this an aneurysm?

How is this real life right now? My dead best friend is talking to me. I must have overdone it on the muscle relaxers.

I finally look at her. "Sex?" I suggest. Megan shrugs as the cigarette ignites from a flick of my lighter. She takes a drag. "Eh, I mean I can take it or leave it. By the end it was like getting plowed by a pillow with a hot dog attached to it." I didn't need that image in my head.

"What's it like being dead?" I ask. Still not convinced this isn't a psychotic break.

Megan puffs on the cigarette some more and answers. "It sucks. I 100 percent don't recommend it. So many things I see now that I didn't before. Which is why I am here."

I grab my smokes from her as she takes out another. I pull a cigarette out and light it. "Why?" I ask. Megan lights her cigarette with fire from her finger and takes another drag.

"You're in trouble Alex."

Oh God, my life is not in a good place. I am hallucinating and talking to it. I take a drag myself. "Let's just say I am in trouble. What would that mean exactly? I'm already convinced I am having a stroke or psychotic break," I say. Megan chuckles lightly, but her face turns serious quickly.

"I'm here to save you from becoming like me. Look at me!" Megan says. She holds up the thick chains around her. "I have heavy chains that are bound to me until I make up for what I've done. I'm doomed. In two years I saved one soul and I've had this conversation with hundreds. Natalie Petosi wouldn't stop tossing back the vodka!" The Speaker of the House is well known for being drunk. It's one of the many focuses of the Conservatives. I don't blame them. Not that I will admit that, but she is of the party, so I have to defend her and her lushyness.

"I don't understand. What because you killed yourself you have to make up for it?" I ask.

Megan throws the cigarette to the floor. "No! The universal will doesn't care about that. It cares that you choose to help and know people as equals." Megan pokes me in the chest. "You don't do that Alex. I didn't either and I am stuck like this, possibly forever. There is still time for you though. You can change and do better." She pleads with me. I can't even fathom why she would be punished.

"What are you talking about? You helped so many women and LGBT people, other minorities—"

I am cut off by Megan. "*All* people should have been who I helped. I only chose people who thought like me. I wished death on those who didn't agree with me! Same as you!" Megan is yelling. I close my eyes in fear.

Megan grabs my shoulders and shakes me until I open my eyes. "You're going to be visited by three ghosts. Each one will be worse than the last. Expect the first at noon tomorrow. If you don't change your ways Alex, you'll be doomed to carry chains of your own for all time," she says as she rattles her chains around her.

I shake free of her grip and scoff. "I'm done with this vodka-induced dream. Go haunt someone else," I say. Megan doesn't leave though. She screams and closes the distance between us. She grabs me by the throat and lifts me in the air. She pushes me against the large window, and I magically get sent through the glass. "Please don't. They'll think I'm a suicide," I plead.

Megan pushes me through and holds me tight. "You can be saved!" she yells through the glass once more. Her body begins to deteriorate and look more like a dried up husk. I grab her arm to support myself and it begins to break. "Three ghosts. Listen to them! Don't end up like me," Megan pleads before her arm breaks and I fall from the top of my building.

I scream as I fall to my death. Before I can hit the street below, I wake up on my couch. I touch myself everywhere to confirm I'm alive. My phone flashes from a *Snapchat* alert, and I see it's Jack with another story update. I ignore the story and send him a frantic chat.

Jack, I know we haven't talked in years, but I need to talk to you. It's important. I'm not sure what's happening. I think I'm in trouble … IDK, please, you're the only one who has ever really listened to me in my life. You can call me if you still have my number.

I drop my phone and walk into my kitchen to grab a Smirnoff screwdriver from my fridge. I pop the cap and I hear Megan's voice whisper, "Three ghosts …"

The next day I wander down to my office after showering and making myself look as perfect as can be. I have to meet with one of the board members and a potential donor. It's a huge deal. Despite being my charity, the board has the final say. My approach has kept them on my side, but maintaining my work has been a struggle. This new donor will be a huge win and allow me to expand and get more board members that I know will vote my way. It will take my stress away … partially.

As I get to my office and head inside, I see a note on my office room door. It simply says meet us at Titanic. It is a new restaurant that opened a year ago. Not sure who the owner is, but they stole Jack's idea. He always wanted to open a restaurant and base it on the Titanic. They are super famous, not just the food, but they are one of the most generous business owners in America. They have a charity attached to the restaurant called White Star. The building is down the street and caters to the homeless, LGBT youth and does after-school programs to help inner city kids avoid the streets until their family can pick them up. I've been trying to meet with the head of the charity for a while now, but when they are free I am busy and vice versa.

As I am making my way out of the office, I see a familiar brunette that I haven't seen in person in years. "Jack," I say very lightly. The man I had wanted to be my husband stands before me.

"Hey Alex. I saw your message. It worried me. I wanted to come down right away," he says.

I don't know what to say. I didn't expect to see or hear from him. A part of me is angry just looking at him because he dumped me or I him. I can't remember anymore. "I'm sorry. I don't know what happened last night. I think I had bad food or maybe vodka. I am sorry. I hope it wasn't too late. I didn't wake you or your boyfriend did I?" I ask.

Jack chuckles. I think he picked up on my veiled

meaning. "No, I'm single. I've been too busy to date anyone. So tell me what's wrong. You seemed really upset. I can only imagine since you texted me," he says. He has a valid point. Aside from yelling at him for involving himself in conservative politics, I've made no effort to talk to him.

I blush and look down. "I—I, I just had something happen last night and it brought up memories. I saw you and I guess in a moment of weakness, I messaged you. How did you know I was here by the way?" I ask. Jack blushes this time and scratches at the floor with his foot. "I kept up with you. I've watched you take on the political arena with your protests. I think you protested a few of my employer's events."

"Yea, I've seen pictures of you in the news with Jason Blackwood. What are you? His campaign manager or something?" I ask.

Jack shakes his head. "Nah, I'm his lawyer, but we became good friends a few years ago."

Lawyer? Jack became a lawyer? "You're a lawyer?" I ask. Jack smiles and reaches into his pocket and pulls out a card. He hands it to me. I take it and look at the card. It says *Infinity* on it. I know them. They represented me more than a few times.

"You work for Infinity? I love them; they've represented me a few times," I say.

Jack smiles. "I know. I had to approve it. I own Infinity. I am not as involved in the day-to-day stuff as I used to be, but I still oversee big cases and requests. I spend most of my time running Titanic and White Star," Jack says as he reaches into his pocket for his wallet and pulls out a card.

How is it possible that Jack owns a law firm that I like, a restaurant and charity I like too? He is part of the Conservative Party! This is insane. I take the card and put it in my pocket. I give Jack a smile. "Wow, you've done an amazing job. I have been trying to meet with the Head of White Star for a while now." Jack blushes and rubs the back of his head. It's an old habit of his when he's embarrassed.

"Yea, sorry. I've just been nervous about meeting you. It was clear you didn't know who I was, but I knew it was you and after how things ended, I was afraid. When I got your text this morning though … I just had to come see you and make sure my old prince is okay." I fight the smile threatening to appear.

"I—I, thank you. I want to catch up more and talk, but I have an important meeting for my charity. I have to go. I'm sorry," I say guiltily.

Jack frowns but nods. "Listen, if you want to meet up, I'm usually in the office at White Star. Please come down anytime. I promise, I'll be there for you," Jack says. I feel tears well up in my eyes. I turn around pretending to lock my office door and thank him and say I'll consider it. Once I can control myself, I turn around and walk out of the building with Jack. I give him a hug on instinct and curse myself as we embrace. Oh my god he smells like vanilla roses. What is that and why does it exist?

Jack walks off to get his car and I head back to my car. When I get to my car, I see my beautiful Tesla's tires are slashed. I wish I could say I am surprised, but given the insanity of last night, I am not. I look and see that Jack is already out of the parking lot. I don't have time to call an Uber, so I have to run to get there on time. Unfortunately the restaurant is a mile away. I start running and curse myself every step of the way. The entire run is filled with rage over the events of last night and now this bullshit.

I finally arrive at the restaurant out of breath and drenched in sweat from the July heat. I curse the universe one more time and walk inside. I see the board member, Ashley. She is with the donor from a high profile electric company. I walk up to them and apologize for being late. They look at me like I am homeless. "I'm sorry for how I look. I had to run here. Someone slashed my car tires," I say before sitting down. They give polite smiles you can tell are filled with judgment. Prissy prudes.

A waiter comes and asks what I would like to drink. I order a vodka martini. While we wait for the drinks, we talk about what we're doing as a charity and our hopes regarding expansion. One of the big goals I have is to see our charity get real living quarters for our homeless rather than cots in an old gym we rent. It is my hope to have an actual apartment building for the homeless where they can get an established address and get started with a job.

Our drinks come back after a few minutes. I go to take a drink and I see an eyeball instead of an olive. I let out a scream and everyone looks at me. I motion toward the drink and the waiter grabs it. "I'm sorry sir. I will get you a new drink. In the meantime, are you ready to order?" the waiter asks.

As I look around to avoid looking at the eyeball, I see a clock in the distance. The hands are on twelve. *Expect the first ghost at noon.* Megan's words echo in my head. The waiter begins to talk to me about different options. His head begins to spin as he talks. It's slow at first and then soon it's spinning like tires on a car going down the highway. No one is reacting to this at all. I am freaking out and making unintelligible words.

Everyone is looking at me like I am the crazy one and this dude's head is spinning like the exorcist! I try to look away and minimize how much of a freakout I'm having, but the rest of the restaurant isn't better. Everything around the dining area turns rotten looking. I see people eating disgusting looking food, people on fire and ooze coming out of the walls like a 70s cliche horror movie. I jump out of my chair which makes it flip over. "I'm sorry but I am having some indigestion. I have to go. Ashley will take care of you and answer your questions." I excuse myself and move to make my way out. The three people stare at me as I walk out of the restaurant. I know I must look insane, but I am fairly certain that is because I am going insane. If no one else saw his head spinning or the other insane stuff, then I don't know what is going on with me.

I leave and pull out my phone and request an Uber. I get an almost immediate response and in a matter of seconds someone arrives. The car looks like crap but I don't care. I just need to get out of here. I get in the car and sit in the back. Before I can even close the door, the car is racing away. "Jesus, can you slow down? I'm not even in the car!" I shout. I peer ahead to try and get a look at the driver's face. He is old and oddly familiar looking. I can't place it.

"I can't slow down, Alex. We have a lot to see before the afternoon is out." The man turns around. "I'm the Ghost of America's past." The ghost smiles and the car doors lock.

I try to open the door but it won't budge. "What do you want? Why haunt me, discount Washington?" I say. It is the first thing that I can think of.

"Oh good you recognized me. I didn't think

your generation cared to remember me anymore because I once owned slaves," the ghost says.

"Oh my god I'm in a car with a racist," I say. I bang on the car which speeds up.

"You know upon my death they were freed right? I'm not saying it was right. It wasn't. The sad alternative though was they were enslaved in worse conditions in their homeland. You people seem to forget they were captured and sold by their own people. Is it right that I and many profited off their labor? Looking back I say *no*. However, I maintain things could have ended up being worse. That's neither here nor there. We are here right now to take you back."

"Let me out you old sociopath! I don't care about the past!" I yell again. The ghost laughs and points to the radio as everything outside begins to blur. The radio number starts changing and lands on 2004. The ghost, who claims to be George Washington, parks outside my parents' house. The doors open and a force throws me out. The ghost gets out of the car gently and walks over to me. For someone who should be centuries old, he is dressed modernly.

"Listen, what is the point of this? You think I'm going to see my father or mother and cry? You have the wrong person. I don't cry," I say defiantly.

Washington stares at me. "Hitler said the same thing. When he saw his mother, it was Niagara Falls," Washington chides.

"That's your example? Hilter killed millions!" I exclaim.

Washington puts his hands up in defense. "Okay dude, this isn't an exact science; not every-one changes, but he did kill himself after the visit from us ghosts, so I call that a minor victory."

Oh great. Suicide is a victory to these ghosts.

The ghost of Washington walks through the door to my childhood home. I walk and bump into a hard wooden door. Washington pokes his head through the door, laughs and says, "I always get the first timers with that one. Let's go. Lots to see." I give the dead man the finger as I rub my head.

I follow Washington into my old home and see my father. He is handing a young me a red, white and blue cupcake. I remember this. Grandma's last fourth of July with us. Then she died. She hid the cancer from us until after the holiday. We thought she would be okay, but the doctors didn't do their procedure right and missed cancer cells in her breasts. It spread and all radiation and other medical options failed. She died the following year just after my birthday in early February.

"Come on Alex! Your mom is getting the tube ready. It's almost dark enough!" my dad says. He has always loved the holiday. I celebrated it with him until I was nineteen. Then I stopped. I just couldn't do it anymore. I haven't seen my family really in years. My brother tries but I don't care to keep in touch with them. They "love" America, but I don't fit into that because I'm gay and don't hold the same values.

Washington and I follow my younger self and my dad outside. Everyone is there. The younger me ran up to my mom and her two sisters. "Come on. Let's see what they are saying," Washington suggests.

I stop him. "Wait! Can't they see us?"

Washington laughs. "No, this isn't real. It's a vision of your memories. We are nothing but ghosts to them." We walk up there and I see my two aunts holding hands. They are super close. That's an odd kind of weird thing for sisters to do. They let go when young me gets closer.

"Oh Laurie, you know you don't have to worry about that. You're my sister and Jennifer is too. You guys may not be able to marry yet, but I'm sure you will one day. Until then, never be afraid to be open and honest. Anyone picks on you, they are getting decked. I know John feels the same. Besides little Alex here would never judge anyone; he loves everything. Isn't that right baby boy?" my mother says to young me.

My aunts are lesbians? Oh my god how did I not notice that? Mom and Dad knew about it then? Then how could they have supported Ace? It makes no sense. The young man gets some small fireworks and runs off into the distance. Dad joins Mom and they watch me light the fireworks and jump around.

"Happy 4th of July Alex baby!" she calls out to me. I see my grandma watching me too. She is sitting down. She doesn't look good. She smiles at me.

The young me runs over to her and hugs her. "Did you see Grandma? It was so cool and bright!"

She ruffles my head. "I got something for you

for later. I know you love the big finales. It's got to wait until all the others are gone, okay? You know it's only the 4th when there is a big finale!" she says. She kisses a very excited me on the forehead.

I feel tears escape my eyes. Seeing my grandma again hurts. I loved her so much and she loved the holiday too. I miss her so much. Washington holds a handkerchief out. "Niagara falls Alex baby," Washington says.

I grab the handkerchief, wipe my eyes and say, "It's not because of seeing my parents or Grandma. I have dust or a twig in my eye or something."

"Yea, and I really have wooden teeth. Let's go. Time to fast forward a little bit," Washington says. We went back to his car. I can't help but wonder when Washignton learned to drive. Once in the car, Washington takes off and the numbers on the radio spin again. This time they land on 2010. It's July 4th again.

This time Washington takes me to a familiar backyard. Jack's. I met Jack in sixth grade. This was the first time I didn't spend all of the 4th with my parents. I remember being nervous about going over to Jack's. I really liked him and I didn't know yet if he was gay. It was late; the final shots of fireworks were going off in the night sky. Jack and younger me were perfectly illuminated by the many colors in the sky.

"Jack, there is something I have to tell you. I don't know how you'll respond, but you're my best friend and I hope that nothing changes," younger me says. Jack flashes a smile at me.

"What's up? Have to be right now?" he asks.

Young me blushes. "It's just, I really like you. I have for a while but I needed to tell you. I'm gay. I think I'm in love with you," young me says. Jack smiles at me. He points up. Young me looks up and in moments Jack is placing a warm kiss on teen-age me.

I can't stop the tears from breaking free from my eyes. "Don't forget. Jack made you like this holiday again. He returned your feelings and reignited the flames of passion and ambition," Washington says. He claps his hands and the scenery shifts to young me at home sending snaps to Jack.

"Okay? And? Yea, Jack made me like the holiday again. He was the first good thing in my life in a while. Sorry I took the death of my grandmother hard. Sorry that my parents' Conservative values made me feel scared as I came to terms with who I was. Why should I apologize for being angry on this day? At my family? This country? All of these things that don't accept me? Tell me that oh great father of our country."

Washington smirks at me and snaps his fingers. Time fast forwards again. The scenery is my childhood home and my parents are cooking. The front door creaks open and it's Jack and me. Oh god no. Not this day. It's the day I came out to my parents. Jack held my hand as I blurted out I didn't care about their politics or religion, and I loved Jack and nothing would change that. My dad made a lame joke. "Oh my God Alex! How could you do this?" Dad storms up to teenage me and points behind me. I remember thinking he was kicking me out. "You tracked in mud! Be more like your boyfriend here and take your shoes off before coming inside from the rain and mud." Dad looks at Jack and smiles. "Jack, we're having homemade hot wings tonight. You in?" he asks as he wraps an arm around him.

I look at Washington. "What's your point man?

Yea my parents accepted me. They still voted for that jackass Daniel Ace! He hates gay people!" Washington sighs and pinches the bridge of his nose.

"He appointed some of the first gay people to high ranking positions and had his UN ambassador put forth motions to decriminalize homosexuality all across the world. I think you're letting media-filled narratives blind you. Was the man perfect? No. Neither was I. Yes history talks about me fondly but that doesn't mean I am sort of god. I did bad too, but the good things I did for the country out-weigh those negative things. It doesn't mean you sweep them under the rug. Remember them so we can learn from history, but while you remember the bad, remember the good too. Ace may not have had your every desire in his interest but does the man you have in office now?" Washington asks.

That was easy. No. Joseph Bodine is an old fool who gropes kids and has clear mental problems due to age. I had no choice but to support that creep though. "I have to support the man. He is a part of the Democrat Party and a legend from the Senate."

Though legend is a stretch. He didn't really accomplish much and stood in the way of progress. He also called people of color "jungle animals" at one point. "That's the problem with today's society. You care about parties. We warned you all long ago that parties would be the end of freedom and look at where you all are now. Two parties run everything." Washington sighs. He snaps his fingers again and the car appears. "Come on. We have a couple of more stops to make," Washington says.

We go to January 2017. Me and Megan are talking about opening up my charity.

"This is so good Alex! We're going to be able to help so many!" Megan says with excitement. I remember this. She was so happy that day. Megan was telling the past me about her idol's email. "I actually got a response from Anya Cordavo. She is such an inspiration being the youngest elected woman into Congress. Sure she doesn't know what a garbage disposal is or that there are two chambers in Congress or that the 2nd amendment is the constitution, but she accomplished so much in so little time." Glad she didn't live to see the congresswoman get on camera and demand the unvaccinated be denied medical care. It was not one of her finer moments and the Conservatives ran with it to demonize my party. Though I did agree about letting the unvaccinated die, it isn't something you say publicly. It's something you do hush hush and then expect the opposite party to get it done.

"I know, it's young people like her that are going to help this country get better. We can take this country back!" the ambitious me shouts. In my defense I was definitely drunk.

I look at Washington. "I suppose you disapprove of my political beliefs?" I ask.

The old President chuckles and says, "Sure on many things but that doesn't matter. What we wanted you and everyone else to do is come together and discuss what needs to be done to ensure the prosperity of the country but also the prosperity of the people. Neither of you political sides remember that and it saddens us to see the country fall so badly. All you all do is bicker when you should be objectively coming together and chasing the path that helps everyone. No one will ever be satisfied completely, and both sides have this my-way-or-go-die attitude that needs to stop." Washington says this matter of factly. I can't say I disagree with what he says. He isn't wrong, but I have to be that way; otherwise nothing will get done. I choose not to respond to Washington and he just points to the car and tells me to get in for our last stop.

I get in the car and go through time to February 2017. Two days after my birthday. I don't want to relive this. "Why are you showing me the day Jack left me like I was trash? I don't want to see this!"

Washington points. "You clearly don't remember what really happened. You stood Jack up on your birthday to protest the construction of a waste-to-power plant which was going to get rid of all landfills, ensure recycling, and eliminate the cost of paying for trash service as it became a part of your electric bill which was reduced. Everyone was going to get a 75 percent reduction in electric cost and you protested it, and your new friends prevented it from happening. In response the electric company raised prices. Remember that summer? Hot. Thousands died because the power was cut and their food went bad or they died of heatstroke.

All because you didn't like the idea of waste being burned even though Sweden does it and you praised them for it."

I look down as the memories fill my head. I hear footsteps and see a very sad and broken looking Jack walk up behind a very busy and focused looking me. He slides his hands around the younger me who is busy looking through papers. "What? What is it Jack? I'm busy," young me irritably says. What kills me is seeing the look on Jack's face. He closes his eyes. I see his lips quiver. He lets go of my younger self and goes over to a chair to sit down.

"I'm sorry. It's just that you've been busy since the election a few months ago. You didn't show up last night for dinner. I had a whole night planned out for your birthday," Jack says, holding back the tears.

Younger me sharply turns around. "I'm sorry that there are more important things than some stupid birthday plans you made. There is a lunatic in the White House and I need him out. Otherwise all the other plans you have for us will never happen. Maybe if you can be a little less selfish and focus on my needs, we can have a happily ever after that you want so badly!"

I can't believe this is me. Did I … did I really yell at him like this? This can't be real. I loved Jack more than anything. I—I couldn't have done this. I can see Jack flinch as the younger me yells at him. Jack excuses himself and walks out of the room. I don't know how the younger me didn't hear or see the tears. Jack walked out of the room crying.

I walk up to myself. "You moron! What's wrong with you? You love him you idiot!" The scenery changes around me and it's a few days later. Jack is packing up his Jeep Gladiator and small trailer. The young asshole me is standing with his arms crossed and pretending not to be crushed. "I hope you have everything. I don't want you coming back here for stuff you forgot. Lose my number, my socials … all of it. I'm done with you. I'm glad you're leaving! I never want to see you again!" the young me lashes out.

Jack says nothing as he walks up to the young me and embraces him in a hug. He holds him tight even though stupid me won't return the hug. He kisses the moron that is supposed to be me on the cheek. "I love you Alex. I hope you find your way back to me but until then … I'll never let go," Jack says. Tears well in my eyes. We always talked about a Titanic romance, and whenever we left one another we always said *I'll never let go*. He lets go of young me and goes to his jeep. He gives one final look at the house and idiot me before driving off.

Present me goes running after the jeep while idiot me stands there in place pretending to be tough. "Jack! Please don't go! This idiot needs you, Jack! Stop! Come back!" I turn and run back to my young self and swing my hand at him to hit him. My hand goes through him. "You're such a pathetic idiot!" I shout at myself.

Washington walks up to me and snaps his fingers. The young me and everything else around me disappears. We are standing in a black void. "I offer you this wisdom Alex. The past is over and can't be changed. Remember who you are and change direction," Washington concludes. Washington begins to dematerialize.

"Wait! What about me? Where are you going? You can't leave me!" I shout. Washington smirks and a word echoes in the void. *Remember.*

I start running into the void. I'm scared. Where do I go? What should I do? Is this some sick cosmic Hell? I keep running until there is nothing solid below me and I'm falling. I start screaming as I fall into the infinite darkness and in moments fall into light and a pool of water.

I kick to the surface of the pool and break through the water. I frantically look around and it's my childhood home. Great. I get out of the water and walk to the back porch to dry off. Rather, strip off my clothes.

Luckily I have a key to the house and am able to unlock the back door and get inside. It doesn't look like anyone is home. Likely Mom and Dad are out buying stuff for the 4th. I find my old room upstairs the same as it was the last time I was here. I grab a towel from my closet and finish drying off before getting old clothes.

I sit on my bed and grab my phone. It somehow survived the pool. I request an Uber and wait. I need to get my car fixed. I hear some noise downstairs and it's obvious someone is home. That or someone is breaking in to murder me and at this point I don't care. I make my way downstairs and see my mom and dad carrying in fireworks and food. I can't help but chuckle at the sight of it. I walk down the rest of the way and sheepishly say, "Hi."

"Alex!" my mom coos. She comes to me and pulls me into a hug.

Dad joins us. "I didn't know you were coming by. It's so good to see you. Are you staying long?" Mom asks.

I look down. "Um, no. I had car issues and this was the closest place. I will try and make it tomorrow though. I know I haven't been around the last few years but I'll try," I say to deflect. I really didn't plan on it but I needed to get out of this situation quickly. I hug my parents. "I love you guys. I know I haven't been around and I've been combative a lot but I do love you guys," I whisper. I mean it too. Still I had some important things to do and protests were being planned.

I part from my parents and get out the door. The Uber is waiting and I get in. I think about where to go and I decide to head to White Star. I need to talk to Jack. I give the address to the driver and we're off in a heartbeat.

Once I'm at White Star, I hesitate to go in. I pace back and forth outside. Partially because I am very nervous about going in but also because of what happened with the ghost. I am freaking out so much. I sit down on the hard concrete sidewalk outside the building. There is a homeless guy sitting there. He looks like a veteran. Great. Warmonger. He deserves to be homeless. The man tries to make conversation with me and I am short and cold to him. There is no reason to help someone who enjoys killing non-white people for a living. "With all due respect, smelly homeless warmonger, go away. Please just die in a ditch and do this world a favor," I say harshly. The look in the man's eyes is broken. I feel pain in my heart from being so mean. I look down and see his name on his military jacket. "I'm sorry, I shouldn't have said that Mr. Jacobs. I am just having a bad day and you're the closest thing to me."

I excuse myself and walk inside the building and take a seat in a chair in what I assume is supposed to be a lobby. I stupidly talk out loud to try and sort my thoughts and people are staring at me. It doesn't help that I look terrible because of the run to Titanic. While I'm sitting there muttering to myself, a woman comes around and grabs me. She ushers me to follow her and tries to calm me down. I can't really tell what she is saying because I am still lost in my thoughts. I've seen two ghosts. Jack magically popped back in my life and I just told someone to kill himself. My life has gotten away from me in the last twelve hours.

"Alex?" I hear an all too familiar voice call. I am broken free of my thoughts and lock eyes with Jack. He walks over to us and thanks whoever the woman was. He grabs me by the hand and walks me away from everyone. Once we settle in place, he rubs my arms and gives me a concerned smile. "Hey, are you okay? You look like you saw a ghost," Jack says. The irony of the cliche is not lost on me.

I bring my hands to my face and cover it. "I don't know if it's stress or the drinking. I'm losing it." I word vomit.

Jack hugs me and shushes me. "Hey, it's okay. Let's go out somewhere and get something to eat and you can just talk to me." I perk up at his words. Jack has always been the best listener. It is probably his best quality. He listens to everything and enters perspective when he feels it's needed.

Jack pulls away and waves to one of his workers. The woman from earlier came over. Jack explains he needs to go with me. She responds that they are having an issue and need him. "Why? What's up?" Jack asks.

"The donors backed out; we don't have enough beds. The donors said they don't like that you support Jason Blackwood." Jason Blackwood. I dislike everything about him and his politics, but it seems heartless to not donate beds for homeless people because of the owner's politics. As long as people in need are being helped, does it matter what they believe? Oh God … Jack said stuff like that to me before we broke up.

Jack turns to look at me. "Give me five minutes

to make a call. I promise, we are going to go out for lunch so you can tell me everything that is wrong."

I sigh and say, "Come on, I'm sure this fine lady can talk on your behalf. I really could use you right now."

Jack frowns a little. "Alex, just five minutes. I promise. Please, just five minutes." I know his heart is in the right place but I can't. My mind is clearing from the desperate need and I'm going to make sure he gives up on me.

I let out a sigh. "I don't think so. Same Jack as always. Everyone else's needs are more important," I begin.

Jack looks at me with hurt. "Just stop. Try focusing on one person or task for a change. Maybe you'll finally succeed," I say. I turn around and walk away before I can take back what I said. This is for the better. Jack deserves better than me. I can't be anything with him. Not even friends. Jack calls out for me despite my outburst. Jack's heart has always been kind. I wish I deserved him.

I walk out of the charity building and go down the alley to cross at the next street. As I walk in the alley, the sky begins to turn dark and the light on the other end of the alley disappears. Oh god no. I turn around and it's black. I turn around again and am face to face with a young blonde woman. "Hi sugar," the woman says before kneeing me between the legs. I groan in pain and hunch forward.

"Why did you do that?" I groan out.

The woman puts a finger to my chin and lifts my head. "Oh I'm sorry. Sometimes life smacks you in the face." A little anger flashes through me.

I smack her hand away. "Fine, smack me in the face, but you hit me in the b—" The woman smacks me in the face pretty hard and I fall down.

She stands over me. "You did give me permission to slap you. How are you Alex? I am the Ghost of America's Present. You might know me as Marilyn Monroe." At least it isn't an old ghost this time. She leans down and grabs me by the shirt and pulls hard to force me up. "I hope you're ready hun. We're going for a trip," she says seductively.

"Go away. I don't care."

Marilyn leans down and forces me up. "Sorry baby, that's not how it works!" she says before shoving me hard. I fall again, but this time I keep falling like when Megan dropped me from my window. I fall through the pitch black darkness until I land on the hard floor in a strange house. Marilyn appears and forces me up. "Try and look a little more lively," she says.

I roll my eyes and dust myself off. "I'm sorry. I just got kicked in the nuts by you. I've been smacked, punched and thrown into an endless pit. I'm a little done with your visit and it's only been five minutes!" I speak viciously at her.

Marilyn rolls her eyes. "Men these days. I swear you act like that was pain. Someone isn't kinky, clearly," I blush and let out a nonsensical groan of frustration.

How is she worse than Washington? *Each ghost will be worse than the last.* Megan's words echo out. I just assumed she meant what they showed me would be worse. Not physical abuse. I wish I was at home drinking. This shit is killing me. My thoughts are broken by the sound of my former assistant Claire. I wonder if this is her home.

We walk toward Claire. She is in her living room with her boyfriend. "So I am going to be at the fourth of July party. I was fired for asking for it off," she says. Tears well in her eyes. Geez, why is she crying so hard? It's just a job.

"Hunny, I'm so sorry. What about your health insurance?" he asks. Well obviously she'll lose it.

"It's gone. I don't know how I'll afford the chemo," she says as she cries into her boyfriend's chest.

Chemo? She has cancer? I look at Marilyn. "What's wrong with her?" I ask.

"She has stage three breast cancer. Don't you remember when she kept wearing head scarves?" she says to me. I think about it but I never noticed.

"I remember her wearing headscarves. I just assumed she became a Muslim." Is that racism? Nah.

Marilyn rolls her eyes. "Men. You don't notice the world around you Alex. You think you're some great virtuous paragon, but you couldn't even be bothered to notice your own employees' medical needs. She never gave any hints?" Marilyn asks. I think back on conversations I had with Claire.

"Hey Mr. Le Dumas, I was wondering if we could add breast cancer to our charitable actions. It affects so many women and even men. I think it could be beneficial and help get more donations," Claire suggested at a meeting.

"I don't think so Claire. I feel for anyone with breast cancer, but there are countless charities about it. I don't think it has room for what I envision," I say coldly. Claire tears up and dismisses herself.

"My God ... I—I didn't know ... I was too focused," I say quietly. We continue to watch Claire and her boyfriend talk until light crying can be heard. The boyfriend tells Claire to wait while he gets the baby. *Does Claire have a kid? I never knew.* A few minutes later he comes back holding a baby that looks like it was just born.

Marylin sniffles and looks at the baby with adoration. "That's why she has stage 3. She knew she had cancer but she was pregnant. She waited until the baby could be safely born but her cancer spread quickly."

I clench my teeth. "Why wouldn't she just abort it and try again when she is healthy?"

Marilyn slaps me across the face. "Killing a life inside of you wreaks havoc on the emotions. Any woman who says otherwise is a monster and any man who suggests it be done is equally a monster. She chose to have a child and let it have life because she knew there was a chance she wouldn't be healthy."

I feel rage build up. "Are you telling me the famous Marilyn Monroe, the woman who showed her tits to the queen, never had an abortion?"

Marilyn flashed a smile. "What I have or have not done is not the point. You don't tell or even get to think she should abort just because it might have been a literal death sentence. She chose. If you're pro-choice, then why can't you respect that? Hmm, little boy?" she says with a smack to my head.

I am tired of being hit. "Listen hooker, you may have been a huge icon because there wasn't a man you turned down, but I am not taking your shit anymore!" I give a shove to Marilyn.

She gives me a smirk. "Strong man and feminist just slut shamed me." She walks back toward me. She pokes me in the chest. I poke her back. This turns into a series of slaps between each other.

"I don't want to fight Alex," Marilyn says. She grabs me on either side of my head and headbutts me. I am completely disoriented by the hit. I trip and fall backwards. The scenery changes around me and I'm in my childhood home. Marilyn drops down from the ceiling and lands next to me. She kicks me in the side.

"God damn it! Stop hitting me!" I shout from the floor.

I get up slowly and Marilyn gives me innocent eyes with a mischievous smirk. "You always protest how women should be strong and independent. Here I am sweetie. Sorry you don't like it," she says as she twirls around in her white dress. Before I can say anything, my entire family makes noise from the living room. It sounds like laughter.

I get up off the floor and walk toward the living room. Everyone is there talking and joking. The menu for Independence day is on. I guess they just watched it. My family always makes the 4th a week-long event. Tonight is the movie and games. Despite being one of the worst video games from the Play Station 1 era, my brother is putting the game in to play it. I used to enjoy watching him struggle to beat the crappy game. I can't help but feel a smile threatening to appear.

"I'm guessing Alex isn't coming?" Lisa asks my brother. Lisa is my brother's wife. She is cool. I've always liked her. She is super mellow but I'm never around the family so I guess I never see her or she me.

Michael grabs the controller and sighs. "Yea. I went to talk to him, but I doubt he will show up. You know how he is. He wants nothing to do with the family since we voted for his sworn enemy."

I scoff. At least he can admit it. Marilyn just watches me. I'm surprised. She hasn't shut up since this started. "You try every year and every year he is too busy. Why do you keep trying?" Lisa asks.

Michael hits buttons on the controller. "He's my brother. I love him and he once loved the holiday and this country so much. I want him to love it again." I feel pain in my heart.

Mom and Dad speak up as well. Not so much to defend me as to echo their hope that I will come back. They mention how they saw me earlier. Thanks Washington. It makes me feel a great deal of guilt. I love my parents even if I can't forgive them for voting for Daniel Ace. I look down at the floor as they continue to talk about me. The things they say and wish pull at my heart and I can feel tears welling in my eyes.

Marilyn walks up behind me and puts her arms

sharply on my shoulders and squeezes. She whispers into my ear. "You've ignored those who love you most and yet here they are, still loving you as if you never left." I look at the screen and see my brother twist and turn through the sky in the terrible Independence Day game. "It's time for us to move on to the next visit." Marilyn says as she squeezes hard on my shoulders again.

I break free from her grip, turn around and shove her. "Not yet. I want to see this part first."

Marilyn smirks. "We have to go Alex!" She shoves me back.

"No! I—I haven't seen this in years. I want to stay," I suddenly say. I can't even tell if it is really me or something else talking.

"You spent years ignoring and pushing them away. Why should now be any different?" Marilyn says and points to the door. "Let's go."

I shake my head and swing my hand through the air. "No, there is one other game we always played … I want to see it."

Marilyn shakes her head. She smiles and comes over to me. She grabs me and forces me toward the door. I struggle against her. I want to stay! I want to play with my brother! I try to push back and Marilyn puts a foot to my chest and shoves me out the door into the void of the ghostly plane. I curse her as I fall into the pitch-black void.

Around me a beautiful house forms. I sit up on the floor I landed on. I look around and wonder whose house this is. "Come on Jack, why won't you go out with me?" Jason asks Jack. I low key growl. That piece of shit doesn't deserve Jack. No one does.

"I am too busy for dating right now. Besides, do you really want to come out during the election?" Jack retorts.

"For you? In a heartbeat." Though Jason can't see it, I can, and I smile huge.

Jack rolls his eyes at his words. "Jason, we've gone over this. You talk a big game, but when it comes down to it, you won't really and I don't feel like getting fired from your campaign when we inevitably get caught together. You'll cut me off completely and I will just be left hurt."

Jack turns and looks at Jason. "I enjoy spending time with you, and you were amazing last weekend but until you're out, I'm saying *no*. I would never ask you to come out until you're ready, but I also don't want to be your secret and then be heart-broken if something goes wrong in your career because of our relationship," Jack explains. I feel my heart stop. Jack was with him? Sexually? I know we haven't been together in years, but I still want him to love only me.

"Hurts doesn't it Alex?" Marilyn says as she walks over to me and crouches down.

I look at her with tear-stained eyes. "Why are you hurting me? What did I do to you?" I ask.

Marilyn holds out a hand and I grab it. She stands up and pulls me with her and says, "I'm not doing anything. You did this. Never forget you pushed Jack away. You loved him but you rejected him for your own personal desires. Now you're crying over a lost love despite him representing everything you hate."

Jack doesn't represent everything I hate. He is one of the kindest people I know. He always has been. The only odds we have are political. "No. I don't ... I don't hate him. I couldn't ... I ..." I trail off as Marilyn stares at me. Jack and Jason talk more in the background.

"I understand. Are you sure it isn't about that guy you used to date? Alex? The one who called me a Nazi who just needed a man to release my tension," Jason asks. I can't help but chuckle at that video I did.

"Jason ... Alex ... well ... he will—" Before I can hear more, Marilyn put her fingers in my ears and starts making noise to block out the sound from them. This went on for a minute. She finally lets go of me and begins to taunt me about how she knows something I don't. I curse at her. Marilyn is really getting on my nerves. I start to understand why she was murdered ... respectfully. She is an icon of Amrican fame.

I look at Marilyn. "Anywhere else you want to take me?" I ask.

"We're not done here. You still have things to learn." I want to ask what but then I see Jack looking through a file. It says Rainbow Lance on it. That's right. I hired his law firm to represent me in a lawsuit filed against me by Jason. I am surprised he is reading that in front of him.

"I can't believe you're suing him. Freedom of speech and all," Jack says.

Jason walks up behind Jack and slides his hands on his hips. He whispers into Jack's ear. "And I can't believe you are defending him after everything he did to you." Jason kisses Jack along the neck.

My ex doesn't react and keeps reading the documents. "I'm not interested. We had fun last week and it was a three time thing. No more." Three times? He slept with Jason on three different occasions?

Jason sighs. "You're no fun. Can we at least play a video game or something?" he asks.

Jack smiles and closes the files. "Sure." The two walk out of the kitchen and head into the living room.

I go to follow but Marilyn stops me. "Time to go Alex," she says.

I look at her with anger-filled eyes. "No! I want to see more of him."

"You can't. It's time to go," she says as she squeezes my wrist and pulls me with her. I fight back and break free of her grip. I run toward the living room so I can see more of Jack.

Marilyn snaps her fingers and everything vanishes. I am in an empty void. Marilyn stands and watches me as I walk around. "Alex," she says.

I stop what I am doing and look at her. "What? What ele do you want to do to torment me?" I ask.

"I offer you this wisdom. Appreciate everything around you; it won't be long before it fades into nothing but a memory," Marilyn says. She begins to fade into the darkness. The solid black under me gives way and once again I am falling through the void. Thoughts of everything I've been shown today flood my mind. A part of me wants to keep falling into the void.

The black void becomes brighter and I am in my office building. It's dark in the office and outside. I look at the clock in my office. It's 10:45 p.m. Not long before it's the 4th.

I search my desk and pull out a bottle of scotch. Jack used to tell me I was so bougie for drinking it when I could just drink whiskey. I pull a glass from the drawer and pour a drink for myself. I think about what the ghost said and showed me. In so many ways I understand what they are saying, but can I change? Do I want to? Everything I lived for has to amount to something. I have so many goals I want to see finished.

I throw back a couple of drinks and decide to pull out my phone. I look at *Snapchat* and see Jack has updated a new story. I look at it. It's him and Jason shooting some fireworks. "Why does he have to be blonde? That has always been your type," I say. It is so obvious in the video and pictures that Jason has feelings for him. You can see it in his eyes.

Jack might have been playing hard with him but I know Jack. He wants the all American family and that blonde prince of the Conservative Party can give it to him. Before I can stop myself, I take a selfie and send it to Jack with a simple, "Miss you." I know I shouldn't have done it but I had to.

I throw back another glass and pour another. Jack responds with a selfie as well. "Figured you hated me still after your outburst." I frown.

I hold up my bottle and take a picture. I sent it with, "Yea and I meant what I said. Still miss you."

I drink more of my scotch. My phone begins to ring and I look down. The number isn't in my phone but I think it is Jack. I answer the phone. "Hello?"

"Are you drinking?" a concerned voice says.

I sigh. "Yes. What are you, my mother?" I say with slight venom in my voice.

"God damn it Alex! You always do this. You get drunk and message me and you mess with my feelings. I can't do this. Leave me alone Alex. If you can't speak to me sober, then don't."

"I need courage to talk to you Jack and I don't have any," I say. I hear a loud crash and what sounds like something breaking. I get up out of my seat.

"Alex ... you're very brave and have lots of courage. You just need—" Jack says.

I cut him off though. "I think someone is breaking in," I suddenly say.

Jack asks me what's wrong and where I am. "I'm at my building. I am going to look," I reply. I look around. I walk toward the noise. I hear Jack telling me to stop and lock myself in my office. I ignore him and continue to walk. He keeps talking to me but it drowns out as adrenaline flows through my body. I see someone in the office. I drop my phone and shout at the intruder. A gunshot goes off and I duck. I didn't think this through. I start crawling through the office to try and find somewhere to hide.

The intruder chases after me which forces me to get up and run. He grabs me and spins me around. I act on instinct and throw a punch at the person who stumbles backwards. I run again and find one of our storage rooms. I slam the door shut, lock it and shove a shelf in front of it. I back up and trip. I fall to the floor. I close my eyes and sigh. "Great. I am going to die," I say. I open my eyes and all I can see is darkness. I sit up and use some random stuff to help myself up. I feel around the dark room for a light switch.

My hand lands on one and I flip it. The lights turn on and I can see everything. Even if the criminal tries to get it, I think I will be fine. To make sure, I decide to push another shelf to barricade the door. It is a little heavier than the last one, so I push harder but it won't budge. I try to put all my strength into it and the shelf moves. I get it in front of the other shelf and push it against the door.

I turn around and that is when I see it. A robed figure standing there. It is holding a scythe. "Jesus … who are you?"

The robed figure holds out its hand and only bones are there. "You know exactly who I am. I am the Ghost of America's future," the being says. I don't remember the final spirit talking in a Christmas Carol. Bastard books and their lies.

"I am not going with you," I say defensively. The spirit snaps its fingers. The room disappears and we are standing in a black void … again. I am sick of being in a void. "Did that work on the other ghosts?" it asks.

"Whatever. Aren't you supposed to be silent? That's how it is written in the book."

The ghost points at me. "This isn't a book." The ghost begins to walk toward me.

I back away. "I don't get it. Washington and Marilyn Monroe were the previous ghosts, but you? You're just a skeleton?"

The ghost chuckles. "Am I? Or am I something far worse? Each spirit gave you wisdom tonight, even your old friend," the ghost begins. "Let's go," it says as it reaches me and takes hold of me.

Black flames surround us and we are transported to the street where my charity is. I see the building. It is in ruins. It looks like it burned down. The ghost points and I walk through the once welcoming door. I look around the charity and the burned ruins break my heart. "What happened here?" I ask.

The ghost walks over broken wood and glass. "With your insistence of being in a bad neighborhood, the charity was finally broken into and burned to the ground. There was only one victim, fortunately," it says. I walk around and go into my former office. The plaque for Megan is black and mostly unreadable. The office isn't much better; there isn't much left. I open one of the burned drawers in my desk. There is a picture of me and Jack. It is burned but it is still in one piece. I pick the photo up. It brings a smile to my lips. That is until I see news reporters show up outside my charity and begin doing a story.

"This is Rainbow Lance, once a strong and aggressive charity that created waves to see the changes needed to empower those who had less. It was in a twist of irony that it was those with less who burned this charity to the ground and murdered—" A strong gust of wind blows and blocks out the sound before I can hear who was murdered. "With the charity gone, it is uncertain who, if any, will resume the once large ambitions of Rainbow Lance."

"Even if my charity burns down. I can always repair it. This isn't going to deter me," I say. The ghost looks at me and stamps its scythe lightly on the charred floor. Dark smoke surrounds us and we are transported to a different place. Instead of the void I now see hospital equipment and staff.

Great. Where are we now? I ask the ghost where

we are and it points to the door. "Go." The door is a room. I walk to it and I can only hear crying. I look in and see a man who looks like he's in his low thirties maybe. Wait. Is that … Claire's boyfriend? I walk in. The sight takes me by surprise and if I could throw up I would. Claire is strapped to machines. She is on a ventilator, bald, pale as the moon and clearly not long for the world.

"Claire, please don't leave me. I need you; our daughter needs you," the man says. I feel my heart drop. She is dying? Because I took away her health insurance? I—I did this! No, how could she have not gotten a job after leaving me?

I turn to the spirit. "There is no way she couldn't get a job after leaving me! She is more than qualified!" I shout.

The ghost snaps his bony fingers and the world around us changes to me in my office. I'm on the phone with someone. "Claire? Sure she worked for me. She was awful. Lazy and stole money from our donations. It's the reason I had to fire her," the vision of me says. The world transforms again and we're back in the hospital watching Claire die.

"Should you refuse to change your path, these

are the actions you'll take. You will cause pain and suffering to multiple people and all because they annoyed you and didn't share your political opinion of the fourth of July and America," the ghost says.

I look away from the spirit and stare at Claire. The heart monitor begins to slow down. The numbers slowly drop. The monitor flatlines and the numbers hit zero. I feel a tear come to my eye and fall. Doctors and nurses run into the room to attempt to revive her, but they fail. I look at the robed being. "Why? How can this be my fault? I am one person," I say in my defense.

"One person with enough ambition can harm more than 1000 men with guns. You fired this girl, you bad mouthed her to other possible employment venues and ultimately because of your cruelty toward her for not aligning with your political views, she died horribly. The cancer may be what killed her, but your cruelty facilitated its progression," the skeletal being tells me. It pokes me hard in the chest. The sharp index finger practically stabbing me. It grabs me. "We've only just begun. Let's go," it commands as it points its scythe and a portal opens.

We walk into the portal and are taken to an extravagant looking room. It's massive. Down in the center of the room at a podium is a middle-aged man. I can't tell who it is. Their face is scarred. Everyone in the room is wearing a suit and has congressional pins. The ghost points toward the man in the middle of the room. "Watch and listen."

"The plot to overthrow America has been quashed. The remaining Democrats will be hunted down and eliminated!" the man passionately shouts. His voice is familiar.

I ask the question in my mind. "Who is this? What happened?"

"What is it you said to him?" the spirit begins. "Oh yes ... Just stop. Trying focusing on one person or task for a change. Maybe you'll finally succeed," it finishes. Those are the words I said to Jack. It dawns on me that this is Jack in the future. I can't believe this.

I focus back on what the future Jack is saying. "The attempt on my life has left me scarred and deformed, but my resolve has never been stronger!" Applause erupts in the assembly.

"To ensure the continuing stability of our great

nation, the United States will be reorganized into the first United Empire!" the man intones. The crowd gives him a standing ovation. What the Hell is going on? Is the United States going to become an empire? How is this possible? I grab the robed ghost roughly and demand to know how to stop this.

"Stop it? Even if I could … no. This is what you wanted. The only difference between what you wanted and this reality is that the emperor of the new United Empire is Jack," the ghost says. There is no way Jack would do this. If there is anyone in the world who loves freedom, it's Jack.

I yell: "He would never do that. He loves this country and believes in the Constitution more than anyone else in this nation! He is objective and would never allow feelings to determine what he does or doesn't do … unlike me … He wouldn't. He can't!" I feel tears breaking free from my eyes.

"Does it hurt? It should. This is your fault. Because of you, Jack decided to see things differently and as you noted, he is objective and with his objective thinking he found a loophole to logically justify his actions to see his ideals come to fruition," the spirit tells me. It snaps its fingers and the world around us changes to an office setting. Jack is sitting in a chair talking to that prick Jason.

Jason says enthusiastically, "We did it darling. With you as the life-long President, this country can finally be restored to its original vision. A hard reset like you talked about for years." Jack takes a drink from his glass. I assume it is scotch or whiskey.

"Believe it or not, Alex is to thank. He told me long ago to focus on one person or task and then maybe I would finally succeed. It was great advice. I focused on returning this country to its original foundation, even if it meant bending some of the freedoms to get it to happen. Tomorrow begins the dawning of a new age," Jack says.

Oh my god. I'm so sorry Jack. I didn't mean this. "Do you miss him?" Jason asks.

Jack scoffs. "No. Alex was an impediment to my goals. I loved him for so long and hoped we could be together again. Thank god I woke up from that," he says with cold malice. My heart shatters from those words. How can this happen to him? I did this?

I look at the ghost. "How can I change this? What do I need to do? I can't let Jack become this way!" I plead.

The spirit stares past me and at Jack. "You can't change it unless you change. Will you? I don't think you will," the ghost says. "We have one more sight to see," the ghost says as he opens another portal and forces me to go through it.

The other end of the portal leads to a graveyard. It's raining out. I see my brother and Lisa standing at a coffin about to be lowered into the ground. Who is it in there? "Is that, is that one of my parents?" I ask. The ghost says nothing. I put my hand to my mouth. I love my parents. I really do. I don't want them to go yet. I begin to walk quickly toward the coffin until I see my parents walk up to join my brother. I look back at the ghost. "Wait, if my family is here then … who's in there?" I ask. I slow my pace and walk slowly toward the coffin.

The ghost follows behind me slowly. It watches as I walk closer. When I get to the coffin, I see a tombstone on the other side. My name is engraved in the stone.

Here lies Alex Mason Le Dumas
02/05/1995 - 10/10/2023
He was passionate about his beliefs.

What kind of engraving is that? No beloved son? Beloved boyfriend? Beloved brother? Nothing? Will no one miss me? Will no one care? I am more than just the work I do. This can't be how my life goes! I can't … I won't allow this! I turn to the ghost and run to it. I bang on its chest and demand it stop this. The ghost shoves me away with an unseen force.

"You want me to stop it? You lived your life for yourself and your ideals and ignored everyone that didn't believe in your beliefs. You chose this life and now you will live with it!" the spirit yells.

"What do I do?" I plead. The ghost smirks and pulls back its hood. An all too familiar face is revealed. Mine. I don't understand.

"I offer you this wisdom Alex. The future is only set if you choose to let it be. Few are given the chance to look beyond the veil, don't squander a gift not afforded to many." The ghost of America's future stamps the scythe on the ground and darkness consumes me.

Once I can see again, I am inside the coffin. I start to bang on the lid and demand to be let out. All I can hear is dirt being thrown onto the coffin. The sound is deafening. I cry and scream and I bang with my fists as hard as I can. I want out. I need to fix this! "Let me out! Let me out! I don't want this! Please! I'll change! I'll change!" The darkness in the coffin consumes me. I feel darkness engulf me. I don't want this to be my future!

STAVE 5

"Let me out!" I yell. I swing my fists and finally they hit air instead of a solid hard lid. I open my eyes and see I am back in the storage closet. Two different sets of gun shots go off.

In a few moments I hear Jack's voice calling for me. "Alex! Alex! Where are you?" I shout back for him and I begin to pull on the shelves I pushed against the door.

I open the door and run out. I see Jack looking around. "Jack!" I shout. He looks at me and we run toward each other.

We embrace in a hug. I pull away from him a little and start kissing him on the cheeks and lips. "Jack ... I'm sorry. I'm so damn sorry!" I say. I kiss him as hard as I can and he returns it with as much force.

"When I heard the shouting and shots, I freaked out. When you didn't answer me back, I was afraid the worst happened. I ran down here as fast as I could," Jacks says between kisses.

"I'm sorry for everything I ever said in the last six years! I love you so much Jack! I can't go another day without you! I promise I will be better. I am done with my bullshit! I will be whatever you need me to be!" I suddenly say.

Jack smiles at me. "I don't want that. I want you to continue to try and reach your goals, just be more objective and kinder, babe," Jack says. He places another kiss on my lips. I smile at his nickname for me. I nod and agree to do better.

After saving me, Jack waits with me until the police come. I have to give a statement on what happened. That night Jackson stays with me in my apartment. He just holds me the entire time. For the first time in six years, I am able to drift into sleep and make it through the whole night.

I'm not done yet. First thing in the morning besides giving more thanks to Jack, I call Claire and tell her she isn't fired anymore. I apologize to her and tell her to take off the holiday and the rest of the week if she wants, but if she wants to keep working at the charity, I want her to stay with a bump in pay. The surprise in her voice is apparent and it makes me happy.

I hang up my phone and smile. Jack is cooking me breakfast. "Happy 4th of July darling!" Jack says.

I wish him the same and say, "Listen, I know you might have plans or something already, but I wonder if you wouldn't mind coming to my parents' house for the 4th fourth? I haven't been there in a while and I want to be there." Jack gives me a smirk.

"Is Mr. Le Dumas asking me to be reintroduced as his boyfriend?" he asks.

I blush. "I would like that but I know maybe we have things to sort out first. I don't want to rush you or anything. I just know they miss you and I would love you to be there," I say, rambling.

Jack smiles and turns the bacon in the pan. "I would love to. I didn't really have plans. Jason invited me over to his family but I'd rather be with you," Jacks says.

He finishes up breakfast and takes a seat with me. He pours us each a cup of coffee. We eat and talk so we can catch up on the last six years. As we finish eating Jack cleans up after us. He eventually sits back down with me and holds my hand in his. "Is everything okay? You seem like Hell itself paid you a visit. I'm glad you see things differently, but I just can't help but ask why." I smile at him.

"It's hard to explain and I'm not sure you would believe me. I'll tell you about it sometime but for now. Let's just say I woke up and am walking away. I know I can still chase after my ambitions but be more objective like you. Will you help me?" I ask him.

Jack smiles. "Always and forever." Jack promises.

After breakfast we go to my parents. Which surprises them greatly. They are happy to see me and seemingly even happier to see Jack. Probably because they always wanted him to marry me. Maybe they will get lucky and see it happen. We have a lot to recover from because of me, but I know Jack is kind enough to help me get there. As day turns to night, fireworks blow in the sky. For the first time in a long time, I feel at peace and great joy. My phone won't stop ringing for the protests, but I put it on silent and leave it in Jack's car.

Tomorrow is going to be the start of a new me that will change the future the ghosts showed me. I won't let that become reality. I don't want to be stuck in a hellish afterlife like that. The road may be rough, but I know Jack will help me be like him. I won't just look to help those who echo my thoughts. Jack does it and I know he will show me how. While I never want to see any of the ghosts again, I wish I could thank them.

The End

www.ingramcontent.com/pod-product-compliance
Lightning Source LLC
Chambersburg PA
CBHW071235170626
46809CB00008BA/3075